DRAGON
Tales

DAV PILKEY

ORCHARD BOOKS / NEW YORK
An Imprint of Scholastic Inc.

A Friend for Dragon, ISBN-13: 978-0-531-07054-3, ISBN-10: 0-531-07054-9.
Copyright © 1991 by Dav Pilkey.

Dragon Gets By, ISBN-13: 978-0-531-07081-9, ISBN-10: 0-531-07081-6.
Copyright © 1991 by Dav Pilkey.

Dragon's Fat Cat, ISBN-13: 978-0-531-07068-0, ISBN-10: 0-531-07068-9.
Copyright © 1992 by Dav Pilkey.

12 11 10 9 8 7 6 5 4 3 2 1   7 8 9 10 11/0

Printed in the U.S.A.   23

ISBN-13: 978-0-545-03953-6
ISBN-10: 0-545-03953-3

First compilation printing, September 2007

The text of this book is set in 18 point Galliard condensed.
The illustrations are watercolor with pencil, reproduced in full-color.

A Friend for DRAGON
Contents

For Cyndi

1
A Friend for Dragon

There once was a blue dragon
who lived in a little house
all by himself.
Sometimes Dragon got lonely.

"I wish I had a friend," said Dragon.
So he went out into the world
to look for a friend.

Dragon went to the woods
and met a small black squirrel.

"Will you be my friend?"
said Dragon.

"No," said the squirrel.
"I'm too busy."

Dragon went to the riverbank
and met a fat gray hippo.

"Will you be my friend?"
said Dragon.

"No," said the hippo,
"I'm too tired."

Dragon went to the pond
and met a slick green crocodile.

"Will you be my friend?"
said Dragon.

"No," said the crocodile.
"I'm too grouchy."

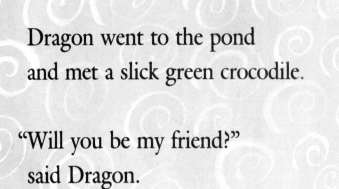

So Dragon sat down under a tree,
still wishing for a friend.
Suddenly, an apple fell
out of the tree and hit Dragon
on the head.

Just then, a little green snake
slithered by. The snake wanted
to play a joke on Dragon.
So it hid behind a rock
and called out, "Hi, Dragon."

Dragon looked all around,
but he didn't see anyone.
"Who said that?" cried Dragon.

"I did," said the snake.
Dragon looked all around again,
but he still didn't see anyone.

"Where are you?" said Dragon.

"I'm right here in your hand,"
said the snake.

Dragon looked at the apple in his hand
and scratched his big head.

"I did not know apples could talk,"
said Dragon.

"Oh, but we can,"
said the snake in the grass.

"Would you like to be my friend?"
Dragon asked the apple.

"Oh, yes," laughed the snake.

"At last," said Dragon.
"A friend."

2
Friends at Home

ragon took the apple home
and built a warm, cozy fire.
He told spooky stories to the apple.
He told funny jokes to the apple.
Dragon talked all day long
and into the night.

"You are a good listener,"
said Dragon. "Good friends
are always good listeners."

19

Dragon fixed a midnight snack.
He mixed cookies, orange juice,
and catsup all together in a big bowl.
Dragon scooped some of the food
onto his plate. Then he scooped
some food onto the apple's plate.

"Just say 'When,'" said Dragon.
The apple did not say "When."
So Dragon scooped some more food
onto the apple's plate.

"Just say 'When,'" Dragon said.
The apple still did not say "When."

So Dragon scooped the rest of the food
onto the apple's plate.

"I am glad that we both like to eat
   so much," said Dragon.
"Good friends should always have
   a lot in common."

Dragon ate up all of his food.
The apple did not eat any food at all.
Dragon was still hungry.
He looked at the apple's plate
and drooled.

"Do you mind if I eat some
of your food?" asked Dragon.
The apple did not seem to mind.

So Dragon ate up all of the apple's food too.

"You are a good friend," said Dragon. "Good friends always share."

3
The New Day

The next morning, Dragon awoke
with the sun.

"Good morning, Apple," said Dragon.
The apple did not answer.
So Dragon went out to the kitchen
and made breakfast.

When he was finished eating,
he tried to wake the apple up again.
"Good morning, Apple," he cried.
The apple still did not answer.

So Dragon went outside for a walk
along the riverbank.
When he came back, he tried to wake
the apple up again.
"GOOD MORNING, APPLE!" he screamed.
The apple still did not answer.

Dragon was very worried.
He called the doctor.
"My apple won't talk to me,"
said Dragon.

"Maybe it's a crab apple,"
said the doctor.

"No," said Dragon. "I think
it is sick."

So Dragon took the apple
to the doctor's office.
They sat down next to a big walrus.

"What's the matter with you?"
asked the walrus.

"It's my apple," said Dragon.
"It won't talk to me."

The walrus stared at the apple
and drooled.

Dragon needed a drink of water.
"Will you watch my apple for me?"
Dragon asked the walrus.

"Sure," said the walrus,
licking her lips.

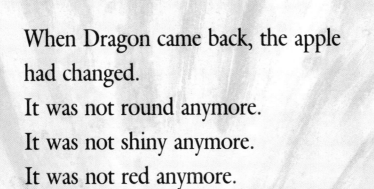

When Dragon came back, the apple
had changed.
It was not round anymore.
It was not shiny anymore.
It was not red anymore.
Now it was wet and skinny and white.

"What happened to you?" cried Dragon.
"Are you all right?"

The little white thing did not answer.

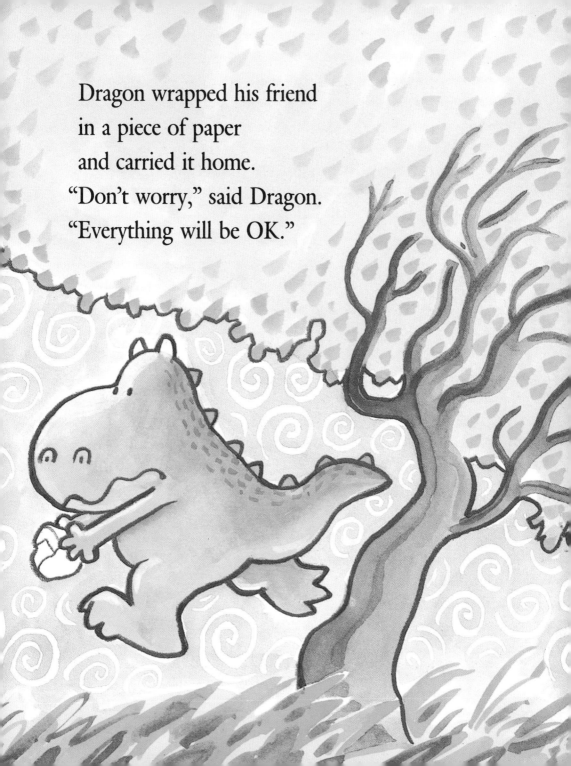

Dragon wrapped his friend
in a piece of paper
and carried it home.
"Don't worry," said Dragon.
"Everything will be OK."

When Dragon got home,
the little white thing had turned all
mushy and brown.

"Are you hurt?" asked Dragon.
The mushy brown thing did not answer.
"Are you sick?" asked Dragon.
But there was no answer.
"Are you dead?" asked Dragon.
Still, there was no answer.

Dragon scratched his big head
and started to cry.

4
Good-bye

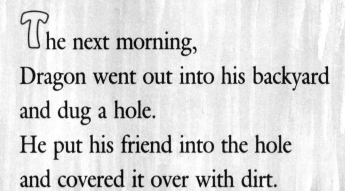

The next morning,
Dragon went out into his backyard
and dug a hole.
He put his friend into the hole
and covered it over with dirt.

Dragon made a sign.
On the sign, he wrote the word
"Friend."

Dragon was very sad.
He cried every day.
He did not want to eat.
He could not get to sleep.
Dragon did not leave his house
for a long, long time.

But after a while,
Dragon stopped being so sad.
He cried less and less.
He began to eat and sleep better.

Still, he was very lonely.

5
Summertime

One day, many months later,
Dragon walked out into his backyard.
He was still feeling lonely.
Dragon sat down under the big tree
growing in his yard.
He wished for a friend.
Suddenly, something fell
out of the tree and hit Dragon
on the head.

It was an apple.

Then Dragon looked up, and smiled.

DRAGON Gets By
Contents

For my old pal, George Hurst

1
Dragon Sees the Day

One warm, sunny morning
Dragon woke up and yawned.
He was very groggy. . . .

And whenever Dragon woke up groggy,
he did *everything* wrong.

First, he read an egg
and fried the morning newspaper.

Then he buttered his tea
and sipped a cup of toast.

Finally, Dragon opened the door
to see the day.
But Dragon did not see the sun.
He did not see the trees or the hills
or the flowers or the sky.
He saw only shadows.

"It must still be nighttime,"
said Dragon.

So he went back to bed.

2
Housework

Dragon's floor was very dirty.
He got his broom and began to sweep.

When he was finished sweeping,
the floor was still dirty.
So Dragon swept again. . . .
And there was still dirt everywhere.

"There sure is a lot of dirt
on this floor," said Dragon.

Dragon swept all morning long,
and into the afternoon.
He carried out wheelbarrows
filled with dirt.

All of his sweeping left
a very big hole in his floor.

Finally, the mailmouse came by.
She looked at all the dirt
outside the house.

She looked at the big hole
inside the house.

"What's going on in here?"
asked the mailmouse.

"I'm sweeping my floor," said Dragon.
"It is very dirty."

"But you have a dirt floor,"
said the mailmouse. "It is made of dirt."

Dragon looked at the hole he had swept,
and scratched his big head.

"Looks like you've made a mess,"
said the mailmouse.

"Looks like I've made a basement,"
said Dragon.

3
Yardwork

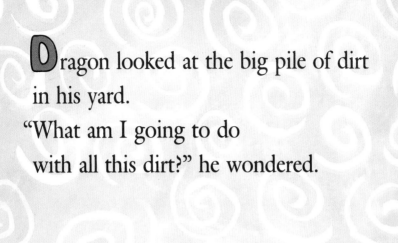

Dragon looked at the big pile of dirt
in his yard.
"What am I going to do
with all this dirt?" he wondered.

He got a shovel
and dug a big, deep hole.

Then he scooped the dirt into the hole.
"Well, that takes care of that,"
said Dragon.

4
Shopping

Dragon looked in his cupboard,
but there was no food at all.
"The cupboard is bare," said Dragon.
"Time to go shopping."

Dragon got into his car and drove.
The food store was at the top of a hill.
It was a very steep drive.

Dragon loved to go shopping.
He was a very wise shopper.
He bought food only
from the five basic food groups:

He bought cheese curls from the dairy group.
He bought doughnuts from the bread group.

He bought catsup
from the fruits and vegetables group.
He bought pork rinds
from the meat group.

And he bought fudge pops
from the chocolate group.

Dragon had a balanced diet.

He had so much food that he could not
fit it all into his car.
"I know what I will do," said Dragon.
"I will eat some of the food now,
and then the rest will fit in the car."

Dragon sat in the parking lot
and started to eat.
He crunched up the cheese curls.
He downed the doughnuts.
He packed away the pork rinds.
Dragon ate and ate and ate
until all the food was gone.
"Burp!"

Now *Dragon* could not fit into his car.
"Oh, what am I going to do?"
cried Dragon.
He thought and thought,
and scratched his big head.

"I know what I will do," said Dragon.
"I will push my car home."

So Dragon pushed his car down the hill.
The car began to roll faster
and faster . . .

and faster . . .

and faster.

Finally, Dragon's car came to a stop
right in front of his house.

All the excitement had made Dragon
very hungry.

He went into his kitchen
and looked in the cupboard.
There was no food at all.
"The cupboard is bare," said Dragon.
"Time to go shopping."

5
Good-night, Dragon

It had been a long, busy day,
and now it was bedtime.
Dragon was very groggy.
So he brushed his head
and combed his teeth. . . .

He watered his bed,
crawled into his plants . . .

. . . and fell fast asleep.

DRAGON'S Fat Cat
Contents

For Thrity
and her cats

One snowy day in January,
Dragon heard a funny noise.
"Meow!"
"That sounds like a cat," said Dragon.

He opened his door and looked outside.
Out in the yard, sitting in the snow,
was a fat gray cat.
"Hello, little cat," said Dragon.
"Come inside and get warm."
But the fat cat did not come inside.
The fat cat just sat in the snow and said,
"Meow."

Later, Dragon heard another funny noise.
"Meow!"
"There's that cat again," said Dragon.

"Won't you please come inside
and get warm?" Dragon asked.
But the fat cat did not come inside.
The fat cat just sat in the snow and said,
"Meow!"

The day passed, and Dragon did not hear
any more funny noises.
When Dragon looked outside,
he did not see the fat cat.
All he could see was a blanket of snow
with a fat lump in the middle.
"Oh, no!" said Dragon.
"Something is not right."

Dragon went outside
and scooped away at the snow.
He scooped and scooped and scooped
until he found the fat cat.

"You are coming with me," said Dragon.
And he took the cold cat inside.

After a few hours by the fire,
the fat cat was warm, dry, and very cozy.
The fat cat sat in Dragon's lap
and purred and purred.

"It is too cold for you
   to go back outside," said Dragon.
"So you will have to stay here with me."
   The fat cat did not seem to mind.
"And if you are going to stay with me,"
   Dragon said,
"I will have to give you a name."
   Dragon tried to think of a name
   for the fat cat.

"I will call you Cat," said Dragon.
Cat was a very good name for a cat.

"If you are going to live
  at my house," said Dragon,
"you will need a bed to sleep in."
  So Dragon took a big brown basket
  and filled it with soft blankets.
  Then he wrote Cat's name on the side.

Dragon put Cat's bed down on the floor
next to his own bed.

"How do you like your new bed?"
Dragon asked.

But Cat was already fast asleep.

And soon, so was Dragon.

3

Problems

Dragon liked living with Cat,
and Cat liked living with Dragon.
But Dragon did not know
how to take care of Cat.
He did not know how to train Cat.

That was a problem.

Dragon did not know what to feed Cat.

That was a big problem.

And Dragon did not know what to do about all the yellow puddles Cat made.

That was a smelly problem.

Dragon tried to teach Cat to use the toilet.

But Cat did not understand.

One day the mailmouse stopped by.

"P.U.!" said the mailmouse.

"Your house stinks!"

"I know," said Dragon.

"My cat has a smelly problem."

"What you need is a litter box,"
said the mailmouse.

"A litter box will make the smelly problem
go away."

"A litter box?" said Dragon.

"That's a good idea."

So Dragon and Cat walked to the highway
and picked up all the litter
they could find.
Dragon put the litter into a box . . .

and placed the box in his house.
Now Dragon's house *really* smelled bad.
Dragon did not know what to do.
"We need to go to the pet store,"
he told Cat.

So Dragon and Cat got into the car
and drove to the pet store.

"I need to buy some cat stuff,"
  said Dragon.
"What's your cat's name?"
  asked the sales pig.
"Cat," said Dragon.
"That's a good name for a cat,"
  said the pig.
"I thought of it myself," said Dragon.

The kind old pig showed Dragon
how to take care of a cat.
She showed Dragon what to feed his cat.
And she even showed Dragon how to get
rid of the smelly problem.

Dragon bought a lot of things for Cat.
He left the pet store with everything
he needed . . .

except for one thing.

4

Left Behind

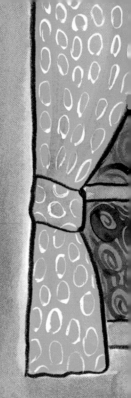

When Dragon came home,
he got his house ready for Cat.
He put out dishes of food and water.
He filled a box up with kitty litter.
And he scattered cat toys all over
the floor.

All the while, Dragon had a funny feeling.
"I feel like I've forgotten something,"
he said.

Suddenly, Dragon remembered
what he had forgotten.
"Cat!" he shouted. "I left you behind!"

Dragon found his flashlight
and went outside to look for Cat.
"Cat! Cat!" he called.
But Cat was nowhere to be found.

Dragon looked and looked
all through the night,
but he could not find Cat.

Dragon sat down on an old crate
and began to cry.
He had lost his cat.

Suddenly, Dragon heard a funny noise.
"Meow!"
Dragon looked around and around,
but he could not see Cat anywhere.
Finally, Dragon looked down
into the old crate . . .
and there was Cat.

But Cat was not alone.
Deep inside the crate,
snuggling close to Cat,
were five little kittens.
"You had babies!" said Dragon.
"Oh, you are a good cat!"

Dragon picked up the old crate
and brought it back to his warm house.

5
Home Again

Later that night, Dragon made up
good names for all of the kittens.
He then made five small beds
and wrote each kitten's name on the side.

Dragon put the kittens' beds on the
floor next to his own bed.
"How do you like your new beds?"
he asked.
But the kittens were already fast asleep.

And soon, so was Dragon.